# ANIMAL +RESCUE

## The Injured Fox Kit

ANIMAL RESCUE

Other titles in the series:

The Unwanted Puppy
The Home-alone Kitten
The Homeless Foal

# ANIMAL RESCUE

## The Injured Fox Kit

## by TINA NOLAN

### tiger tales

# tiger tales

5 River Road, Suite 128, Wilton, CT 06897
Published in the United States 2017
Originally published in Great Britain 2007
by Little Tiger Press
Text copyright © 2007, 2017 Jenny Oldfield
Interior illustrations copyright © 2017 Artful Doodlers
Cover illustration copyright © 2017 Anna Chernyshova
Images courtesy of www.shutterstock.com
ISBN-13: 978-1-58925-499-2
ISBN-10: 1-58925-499-6
Printed in China
STP/1000/0198/0318
10 9 8 7 6 5 4 3 2

For more insight and activities, visit us at www.tigertalesbooks.com

This series is for my riding friend Shelley,
who cares about all animals.

# ANIMAL MAGIC
## RESCUE CENTER

## MEET THE ANIMALS IN NEED OF A HOME!

### GORDON

A handsome black-and-white goat. He's sleek and silky and very smart! Good company for ponies out to pasture.

### JASPER

Jasper is a three-year-old brown and white terrier who would love a new home in the country. Lively and lovable.

### PETAL

An unwanted bunny with beautiful black-and-white markings. She's sweet and looking for her forever family.

SITE SEARCH

 **NEWS**

 **HELP US**

**CONTACT**

**DONATE!**

## LILY AND TULIP

Friendly, playful, and affectionate kittens who would like to be adopted together. Aren't they adorable?

## VIOLET, TIMMY, AND RINGO

This trio is ready to go! Violet loves to cuddle, Timmy is a shy little thing, and Ringo has a twinkle in his eye.

## MILLIE

Millie's life has been hard, but despite that, she is patient and kind. Can you give her the home she deserves?

# Contents

Chapter One
A Troublesome Billy Goat     11

Chapter Two
A Cry for Help     20

Chapter Three
Exciting News     31

Chapter Four
Gordon Runs Wild     42

Chapter Five
The Bad News     54

Chapter Six
The Sad Truth     63

Chapter Seven
Breaking the Rules     73

Chapter Eight
A Genius Idea     85

Chapter Nine
A Magical Good-bye     95

Chapter Ten
Tracking Copper     107

Chapter Eleven
A Family Reunion     112

### Chapter One

# A Troublesome Billy Goat

"Gordon is a black-and-white goat," Caleb Harrison typed. "He needs a home with high fences and plenty of grass."

"Put 'handsome' in front of 'black-and-white,'" Ella told him. "'A handsome black-and-white goat.' We have to make people really want to adopt him!"

"Okay," Caleb said. "H-a-n-d-s-o-m-e." He'd already scanned a picture of Gordon into the computer. Now it was up to Ella and him to write a description.

"What else? Can we say he's great with ponies and horses?"

"Good idea. How about, 'Good company for ponies out to pasture.' That should make horse people look twice."

As Ella and Caleb worked at the computer in the office at Animal Magic Rescue Center, their mom, Heidi, was busy in the exam room next door. She was admitting a young, abandoned terrier named Jasper.

"Just look at this poor dog's teeth!" Mom gasped.

Joel, the center's assistant, peered into the terrier's mouth.

"There's a build-up of plaque and gum disease like you wouldn't believe," Mom complained. "And Jasper can't be more than three or four years old."

Joel nodded. "I can see. It won't be long before his teeth begin to fall out."

"Not if I have anything to do with it," Mom said firmly. "Let's microchip him and give him his shots, then get straight to work on some dental hygiene before it's too late!"

But the little white and brown dog had other ideas. When they tried to look into his mouth again, he squirmed and wriggled, yelped and barked.

"Calm down," Joel said. "We're trying to help here."

"Woof!" Jasper complained. "Woof! Woof!"

"Hey, do you mind—I can't hear myself think!" Caleb objected. "What else can we say about Gordon?" he asked Ella. "Come on. You're good at these descriptions."

"Okay. 'Gordon is a handsome black-and-white goat,'" she repeated. "'He's sleek and silky and very smart!'"

From the moment their dad had brought Gordon into the rescue center the day before yesterday, Ella had adored him.

"The owners can't handle him anymore," Dad had explained. "They say he eats everything in sight and keeps escaping from his field!"

Mom had shaken her head and sighed.

"He's going to be a hard one to find a home for," she'd predicted. "These days, people want nice, quiet ponies and donkeys, not noisy goats. Especially a billy goat."

But Ella had fallen in love the moment Gordon trotted into the stable. "He's beautiful!" she'd sighed, putting her arms around his neck and letting him nuzzle close. "How could anyone possibly not want an animal as adorable as Gordon!"

"Dad, why don't people want goats?" Ella asked.

She'd left Caleb in the office, hard at work on the computer. Crossing the yard, she found her dad mucking out the new

stables. It was early evening. The sun was
setting over the golf course beyond the
river at the back of Animal Magic.

"Because goats are greedy, noisy,
and bad-tempered." Her dad grinned
and winked at her as he pushed a
wheelbarrow out of the stable block.

"Shhh!" Ella looked astonished. "Don't
say that. Gordon can hear you!"

Her dad laughed. "He doesn't
understand—he's a goat, remember?"

"Goats are clever," she protested,
blocking his way. "For all we know,
Gordon can understand every word
you say!"

"Okay, Gordon, I didn't mean it!"
Dad called over his shoulder. "I love you
anyway!"

"You do?" Ella checked.

He nodded. "Even though he just butted me while I was mucking out his stall."

"Really?"

"Really! Right on my leg—pow!" Gingerly Dad rubbed the spot.

"Oh—I'm sure he didn't mean to," Ella said hastily. Now she wanted to check on Gordon and make sure he hadn't hurt himself. She sidestepped her dad and slipped into the stables.

"He meant it all right," Dad muttered as he pushed the wheelbarrow across the yard. "And I have the bruise to prove it!"

"I love you, Gordon!" Ella soothed the goat's hurt feelings. She saw the bucket of fresh green cabbage leaves in the corner of his stall. "And so does Dad. He's given you all this yummy food!"

Gordon nuzzled close to Ella. His dark brown eyes were fringed with lush white lashes. His black face had two beautiful white stripes running down its length.

"You're so silky smooth," Ella whispered. She petted his neck, then bent to pick a choice cabbage leaf from the bucket.

With perfect timing, Gordon lowered his head and gently butted her in the back. Ella fell forward into the straw.

"Hey!" she cried. "I've been sticking up for you, and now you go and do that!"

Picking herself up, she glanced at Gordon, who stared at her with twinkling eyes. The corners of his mouth were turned up in what Ella could have sworn was a smile.

"Gordon!" she cried. "You're trouble!"

He flicked his long, white ears and did a little hop and skip in the straw.

"But you're still my favorite!" Ella grinned. "No matter what people say about you, you're still totally ... well, trouble is all I can say!"

## Chapter Two

# A Cry for Help

Ella bolted the door of the stable block, then set off across the yard. An owl roosting in the trees beyond the golf course hooted in the twilight.

"Dad, did you check the side gate?" she called across the yard. There was no answer, so she decided to do it herself. Checking the gate was part of the evening routine at Animal Magic. Often people dumped their unwanted pets there just as it was getting dark.

Sometimes there would be a note taped to a cardboard box—"Her name is Molly. She's eight weeks old. Please take care of her." And inside the box there would be a lonely, frightened puppy.

But most of the time there was no note, no explanation—nothing except an abandoned cat in a basket, or a shivering pet rabbit, sometimes even a snake, and once, earlier in the summer, a bright red and blue macaw, complete with cage.

Ella opened the side gate that led out onto a narrow road. She looked up and down. Tonight there was nothing to see, but as she went to close the gate she heard something—a faint noise carrying on the breeze. Ella went out into the road and listened hard.

Maybe she was wrong. What she'd

thought was the cry of an animal in distress had probably been nothing after all. Once more she turned to close the gate.

Then she heard it again—a high-pitched call. It was definitely an animal; she was sure this time. The sound came from somewhere in the horses' field at the back of the rescue center. Very high, very frightened, and helpless.

Without stopping to think, Ella took off down the road. She climbed the fence into the field where their next-door neighbor, Mrs. Brooks, kept Buttercup and Chance, the foal. She saw the mare standing alert at the top of the field, staring down the slope.

"It's okay, I'm on it," Ella muttered to the two horses. She made her way quickly down the hill until a shout came from the Brookses' yard.

"Ella, what are you doing?" Mrs. Brooks called. "It's going to be dark in a minute."

Of course Mrs. Brooks would have her eagle eye on the field! Ella sighed, then trotted up the hill to explain. "I thought I heard something down by the fence."

"What kind of thing? Do you think thieves are trying to steal the horses? Wait here. I'll go and get Mr. Brooks."

"No, wait!" Ella should have guessed that their nervous neighbor would jump to the wrong conclusion. "It's nothing like that. The sound I heard was like a small animal in distress—maybe a kitten or a puppy. Who knows— the poor thing might have been dumped outside our gate a while ago. Maybe the animal made its way down toward the river."

"Oh, I see. You're on a rescue mission." Mrs. Brooks relaxed. "But are you sure you should go alone?"

"It's okay, honestly." Ella had no time to lose—the light was fading fast and the poor creature, whatever it was, was still crying out for help. "I'll be quick."

"Oh, yes, I hear it!" Mrs. Brooks nodded. "I'll run next door and tell your mom and dad."

Escaping at last, Ella turned and sprinted down the hill. The noise drew her to the fence, where she stopped and knelt down on her hands and knees.

"Why does it have to be so dark?" she muttered, pushing through long grass. The cries had stopped, but she could hear movement in some low thorn bushes beyond the fence, on the sloping bank leading to the river. Ella crawled under the strong wooden fence toward the bushes.

"Oh!" she gasped.

She saw amber eyes flash in the dark shadows, then vanish.

Ella ignored them, and down below her, the high, frightened cry began again.

She crept toward the sound, which was almost lost in the rushing water. She was about three feet from the river, straining to hear. What tiny creature was it that had found itself in such danger?

Ella's foot sank into boggy ground and she almost lost her balance. The water raced by, fast and dangerous.

"Whoa!" she muttered, stooping again and parting the long grass by the river's edge.

The creature's cry was frantic. Ella saw another pair of bright eyes. She heard howls of pain. Reaching to rescue the small, trembling animal, she found that it was trapped by its leg in a short coil of rusty barbed wire.

What now? If she tugged at the wire, it would only cut deeper into the flesh. "Shhh," she whispered. "Don't struggle. I'm here to help."

As the creature wriggled between her hands and cried, Ella could see a white flash of fur on its chest. Maybe it was a puppy, although it was too dark to see clearly.

"Ella, where are you?" a voice yelled from the horses' field.

"Down here!" Ella recognized her mom's voice. "By the river. I need help!"

"I'm on my way. Hold on."

"We'll soon get you free," Ella whispered, petting the soft fur.

Then a flashlight beam cut through the bushes, and Mom appeared. "What do we have here?" she asked as she climbed the fence and scrambled down the bank.

"I think it's a puppy." Ella held on as gently as she could. "He's gotten his leg caught in some barbed wire. We need to loosen it without hurting him any more."

"I'll use my fleece jacket," Mom decided, quickly pulling the long sleeves over her hands to protect them. "Hold him still and shine the flashlight with your other hand. I've found the end of the wire. Now I'm going to unwind it from around his leg. That's right, Ella. You're doing a great job."

Ella winced as the creature cried. At last her mom got rid of the tangled wire.

"Now let's take a look at you, you poor little thing," Mom said.

"Oh, his leg's bleeding really badly!" Ella cried.

Her mom examined it quickly. "Looks like he's already lost a lot of blood. He's pretty weak."

"Quick, let's get him home!"

"Wait a minute, Ella. Can you shine the flashlight on his face?"

Ella did. The beam of light showed a brown face, a white muzzle, and big, pointed ears with black tips.

"This isn't a puppy," Mom told Ella, studying the young creature.

"Let me see, Mom." Ella was torn between taking a close look and getting back to the animal hospital. She led the way up the bank and into the field.

"You've rescued a fox kit," her mother said, cradling the creature in her hands.

"Wow, I've never rescued one of those before!" Ella gasped.

"He's probably about six weeks old. And I'm sorry to tell you this, but at this moment I'd say his chances of survival are pretty slim."

"You mean he might die?" Ella gasped.

Her mom nodded.

As they ran up the hill, a pair of piercing bright eyes watched from the undergrowth.

"Come on, Mom, we have to hurry!" Ella cried. "He can't die. Not now—we won't let him!"

## Chapter Three
# Exciting News

"Okay, I've stopped the bleeding and put five stitches in the leg wound." Back at the hospital, Mom worked fast. Joel stood by with the tools she needed.

"We'll put him on a fluid drip overnight and check his temperature every hour. That way, we'll know whether any infection has gotten into the wound."

Ella hovered close by. The fox kit was tiny and weak. He lay on his side with his eyes almost shut, taking shallow breaths.

"Where will you put him?" she asked Joel, who was setting up the drip.

"In the kitten unit," Joel said quietly. "We'll use a heat lamp on him to keep him warm and cozy."

"Poor little thing!" Ella breathed. Her heart went out to the helpless baby. "Can I stay up and keep an eye on him?" she asked her mom.

Mom shook her head. "That's Joel's job."

"But Joel will be too busy to sit with the kit all the time. What if he suddenly gets worse?"

"Ella, you can't do any more than you've already done," Mom insisted. "And you need to get to bed. Come on. Let's go back to the house."

"But Mom!" Ella protested. The
kit's high-pitched cries for help still
rang in her ears. How could she possibly
sleep, not knowing if he was going to
pull through?

"Don't worry, Ella. I promise I'll
take good care of him." Carefully Joel
picked up the kit and carried him into
the cat area. The door swung closed
behind him.

"Let's go," Mom said again.

Silently, her head hanging, Ella
followed her mom across the yard and
into the house.

"I'm going to call him Copper," Ella
told Joel. She'd been up early and out in
the cat area, still in her pajamas, before

anyone else was awake. Now she gazed anxiously at the tiny fox kit.

"Copper suits him," Joel agreed.

The cub seemed to be breathing better and was fast asleep.

"How is he?" Ella held her breath and waited for Joel's answer. It was as if she'd held it all night, hardly sleeping, wondering how the fox kit was doing.

"He's hanging in there," Joel said. "His temperature is normal. The wound is clean."

"So he's going to be okay?"

Joel let a few seconds go by before he replied. "We have to wait and see."

"Meaning?"

"Meaning—we just have to wait and see!" Joel smiled kindly. "Copper is a fighter, I will say that."

As if to prove it, the little kit slowly opened his eyes and tried to raise his head. Weak as he was, he looked around, then pulled at the tube attaching him to his drip.

"Okay, little fella, we can take this away now if it's bothering you." Quickly, Joel disconnected the tube.

"Good job, Copper!" Ella breathed, bending over the unit. "You made it through the night!"

The kit looked up at her with his big, light brown eyes. They were flecked with gold.

"You're beautiful!" Ella whispered. "Your name is Copper, and you're going to be fine!"

"Hey, Ella, why are you still in your pajamas?" Annie Brooks asked. She'd come to the house at nine o'clock, looking for Ella. Caleb had told her to try the cat bay.

"Why? What time is it?" Happily bottle-feeding a tabby kitten, Ella glanced up at her friend.

"Time you got dressed," Annie grinned. "Mom said that she saw you in the field last night. She said you were on a rescue mission. What happened?"

Ella gently put Lily the kitten back into her cozy cage. Lily snuggled up to her brothers and sisters. "I'll show you," Ella said, her brown eyes sparkling as she led the way to Copper. "This is what happened!"

"A baby fox!" Annie exclaimed, her

own face lighting up with delight.

Copper lay curled up, blinking sleepily. His little pink tongue peeked out of his mouth, and he licked his lips.

"What's wrong with him? Where did you find him? Oh, he hurt his leg!" Words tumbled out of Annie's mouth.

"Shhh!" Ella warned. "Don't scare him."

Annie crouched level with Copper and gazed at him through the clear sides of the unit. "I've never seen a fox up close before," she said. "He's amazing."

"And he's hungry," Joel interrupted, presenting Ella with a syringe filled with warm milk. "Here's a chair for you. Would you like to try feeding him?" he invited.

Nodding eagerly, Ella lifted Copper onto her lap. He felt warm and soft. His pointy tail with its white tip brushed against her hand. "Do I give it to him the same way I do with the kittens?" she asked Joel.

"Yes. Don't be scared. Just slide the dropper into his mouth and let the liquid trickle in."

Nervously, Ella gave Copper the milk, relaxing as the kit tasted the first drops and then swallowed eagerly.

"Oh, wow!" Annie sighed. "He's so cute!"

Copper gulped greedily until the syringe was empty.

"Phew!" Ella was relieved. "He can't be that sick," she grinned.

"No, there's nothing wrong with his appetite," Joel agreed. "Let's check his temperature and pulse."

The girls watched as Joel performed the checks and then put Copper back in the unit.

"Hmm," he murmured as he read the thermometer.

"What?" Ella and Annie asked.

"His temperature is a little high. It may be nothing to worry about, though."

Just then, Caleb hurried into the cat area. "Who says people don't like goats?" he cried, spying Joel, Ella, and Annie gathered by Copper's unit. "Hey, cute fox kit," he said casually.

"Shhh!" Ella said. "Don't scare him."

Caleb ignored her. "Anyway, I just got an email from a couple who want to see Gordon! It's amazing—he hasn't even been on the website for 24 hours!"

"Shhh!" Ella said again, dragging her brother down the row of cat units then out into the reception area. Annie sneaked one last look at Copper, then followed.

"Mr. and Mrs. Wesley want to give Gordon a home!" Caleb insisted. "Mom was wrong—people *are* interested in goats. The Wesleys say Gordon would live in a field with their pony named Henry. How cool is that?"

"Very cool," Ella agreed. "When are they coming to see him?"

"It's Saturday, so they can come today," Caleb replied. "It's a record—we found a home for a goat in less than a day!"

Annie watched Caleb and Ella do a high five by the reception desk. "Aren't you counting your chickens before they're hatched?" she asked cautiously.

Ella frowned. Caleb shook his head. "No way!" they both said.

"Be careful, Annie—you're starting to sound like your mom," Caleb added, dashing off to find his dad and tell him the good news.

## Chapter Four
# Gordon Runs Wild

"Yes, I'm afraid Copper has developed a fever," Mom told Ella and Annie later that morning. The latest temperature check had confirmed Joel's earlier suspicions.

"That's not good, is it?" Annie asked.

Ella crouched down to take a closer look at the kit.

"No, but it often happens when there's an open wound where the dirt can get in. No matter how much we clean it, there's still a risk."

"Will you give him antibiotics?" Ella asked anxiously. Copper was lying on his side, his legs outstretched, his body limp.

Her mom nodded. "And plenty of fluids. He's just had a drink of water, so what we need to do now is leave him alone."

"You hear that, Copper? You have to stay here and rest," Ella whispered. Her heart sank at the latest news. Would this lonely, small creature find the strength to stay alive? "We'll take care of you as best we can," she promised, leaving him to sleep.

"Okay, Gordon, it's time for your beauty treatment," Ella said, peering into the goat's stable. The girls were armed with sprays, brushes, and combs and were doing their best to stay busy and not worry about Copper.

Gordon glanced over his stable door. He snickered when he spotted the brushes.

"We have to make you look good for your visitors," Ella explained. "You're a handsome boy, and you need to impress Mr. and Mrs. Wesley by looking your best."

"He's a goat," Annie pointed out. "He doesn't understand what you're saying."

"Yeah, that's what Dad thought, but he still managed to hurt Gordon's feelings. Gordon's really clever, aren't you, boy?" Ella opened the stable door and went in. Annie followed close behind.

The goat stepped back to take a good look at the girls. He rolled his yellow eyes at the white plastic bottle that Ella held in her hand.

"It's detangler and conditioner," she explained. "I spray it on your coat, like this."

Squirt-squirt! A fine mist landed on Gordon's back. He threw back his head and brayed.

"He doesn't like it!" Annie gasped, dropping her brush in surprise. As she knelt to pick it up, Gordon did one of his little head-butts. Annie sprawled forward into the straw.

"Oops!" Ella giggled. "Are you okay?"

Frowning, Annie stood up. "Are you sure this goat is safe?" she asked.

"Of course! Watch." Confidently, Ella

stepped up to Gordon and began to
brush his long, smooth coat.

Gordon flinched and lowered his head.

"Watch out!" Annie warned.

The goat had his eye on the stable
door. He stamped his feet and snorted.
Then, with one sudden, mad dash,
he charged.

"The door—I didn't lock it!" Annie
cried.

Ella threw herself at the door, but it
was too late. Gordon reached it first,
barged through, and fled from the
stables.

"Oh, no!" Ella gasped. Picking herself
up, she ran after him.

Gordon was fast. He raced across
the yard, up onto the manure pile,
and over the fence into Buttercup and

Chance's field.

"Oh—oh!" a desperate Annie cried, chasing after Ella. "Mom will be so angry if he scares the horses!"

By this time, Caleb had come running, and Mrs. Brooks had flung open her back door. Hearing the commotion, a puzzled Mom and Dad emerged from the house.

"Gordon escaped!" Annie shouted. "Ella's gone after him!"

"Oh, great!" Caleb muttered. "The Wesleys are on their way to see him right now."

"Ella, wait! Take a harness!" Dad yelled.

But Ella was already vaulting over the fence in hot pursuit of the goat. Gordon was charging across the lush green field, kicking up his heels and making a terrible racket.

"Get that horrible thing out of my field!" Mrs. Brooks wailed as she stood by her fence.

"Uh-oh!" Mom sighed. Just when they thought they'd gotten Mrs. Brooks on their side at last, something like this had to happen. "Now Linda will be up in arms against Animal Magic all over again."

"Don't worry. I bet that the Council has already decided whether or not to keep us open," Dad assured her. "We're waiting for a letter in the mail any day now, remember?"

"Yes, but...," Mom muttered, shaking her head.

Meanwhile, Ella chased Gordon up and down the field. "Come back!" she called, waving her arms and skirting around the back of Buttercup and Chance.

Buttercup whisked her long, white tail
and laid back her ears. Little Chance
stuck close to his mother's side.

Gordon cantered on, kicking up his
heels and enjoying his freedom. He felt
the breeze on his face and the sunshine
on his back—no way was he planning
to give up!

"Come here!" Ella yelled again as
Gordon doubled back and galloped up
the hill.

Caleb stood next to the fence,
watching. "She's never going to catch
him," he told his dad.

"Annie, how did that creature get into
my field?" Mrs. Brooks demanded as
soon as she spotted her daughter in the
yard next door.

"It was my fault," Annie confessed.

"I didn't lock his door."

Caleb shrugged, turning just in time to see a red car enter the yard. He groaned as he saw two people climb out.

"Stop him!" Mrs. Brooks cried as Gordon sprinted straight toward her fence. She cowered against an apple tree and closed her eyes.

"...Mr. and Mrs. Wesley!" Caleb said, doing his best to smile at the visitors.

A small, middle-aged man in a gray jacket and jeans, and a taller woman wearing jeans and stable boots stared at the chaos.

"We came to see the goat," Mr. Wesley began, "but maybe this isn't a good time?"

Just at that moment, a galloping Gordon

made a great leap over Mrs. Brooks's
fence into her yard. He'd spotted
marigolds and daisies, and better yet—
lettuce and peas growing in neat rows.
What a treat!

"Help!" Mrs. Brooks cried from under
the apple tree. "Shoo, you horrible
thing! Leave my lettuce alone!"

"Gordon, come back!" Ella cried,
staggering breathlessly up the hill.

The goat munched and trampled,
then munched again.

"Is that him?" Mrs. Wesley stepped up
to the fence and peered with horror at
Mrs. Brooks's ruined garden.

Gordon glanced up. He had a
mouthful of crunchy young lettuce and
a mischievous look in his eye.

"That's him," Caleb groaned, as

## ✥ Gordon Runs Wild ✥

Mr. and Mrs. Wesley shook their heads.

"Oh, dear!" Mr. Wesley turned to his wife. "Gordon seems to be more of a handful than we expected."

"Yes," Mrs. Wesley agreed. "We'd better go home and talk about it."

"Terrific!" Caleb groaned, as he watched Gordon's potential owners walk quickly away.

### Chapter Five
# The Bad News

"You win some, you lose some," Dad
told Caleb as the Wesleys' red car drove
slowly out of the yard. "There's never
any guarantee that things will work out
as planned."

But Caleb was furious. "How come
Ella isn't in trouble?" he wanted to
know. "If she and Annie hadn't been
messing around in Gordon's stable, this
would never have happened."

Annie cringed, then crept quietly away.

"We weren't 'messing around.' We were grooming him!" Ella yelled from the yard next door. Red-faced and breathless, she was still trying to corner the runaway.

"Try this." Mom passed Gordon's bucket of cabbage leaves over the fence, together with a harness and lead rope from the stables.

Ella held out the tempting food. "Yummy cabbage!" she cooed.

Gordon raised his head and flared his nostrils. He moved closer to the bucket, his top lip quivering. As he stretched his neck to grab a bite, Ella quickly slung the rope around his neck.

"Good job," Mom said as Gordon let out a loud, surprised bray.

"Get him out of here!" Mrs. Brooks

screeched. "Just look at the mess. He ruined my lettuce patch!"

Tugging with all her strength, Ella managed to lead Gordon up Mrs. Brooks's driveway.

"Gosh, you're stubborn," she muttered, steering him next door.

Gordon's hooves clattered across the yard toward his stable.

"Be careful not to get behind him," Dad said. "He'll kick you if he's given the chance."

Huffing and puffing, Ella finally got the runaway goat back into his stall.

"What now?" Caleb demanded. "The Wesleys will never adopt Gordon after what they've just seen!"

"I'm sorry!" Ella gasped. "That wasn't supposed to happen!"

# 🐾 The Bad News 🐾

"Okay, let's all calm down," Mom said. "I'm sure there'll be other possible owners. If you ask me, our main problem right now is not finding a home for Gordon. It's Mrs. Brooks and her lettuce patch."

"Don't worry. I'll go talk to her," Dad volunteered.

"And I'll get back on the website and start all over again," Caleb muttered, frowning.

In the quiet that followed, Mom looked at Ella. "Are you okay?"

Ella sniffed and nodded.

"Disappointed?"

She nodded again.

Mom smiled and gave Ella's hand a squeeze. "Come on. Let's go and check on Copper. It's time to feed him again."

"His temperature's still high but his pulse is normal," Joel reported as Ella sat down with the fox kit on her lap.

Mom handed her the syringe. "Don't worry. The effect of the antibiotics will soon kick in," she promised. "Try to get him to drink as much of this milk as you can. It'll keep his strength up."

Ella nodded, then gently opened the kit's mouth. He stared up at her with his golden brown eyes as she slid the tip of the syringe into his mouth. "There!" she whispered. "It tastes good, doesn't it?"

Copper gulped, then swallowed.

"Good boy. Are you nice and warm in your bed?" Ella talked softly to Copper as he ate, being careful not to touch his injured foot. "He's drinking well," she told her mom.

"It looks like he's getting better." Mom gave a satisfied nod, then went to take a look at the five kittens in the nearby unit. "Have you given Coco's kittens names yet?" she asked Ella.

"Lily, Tulip, Violet, Timmy, and Ringo." Ella ran through the names. "Caleb already put them on the website." She gave Copper the last drops of milk, then cuddled him close.

Her mom glanced at her over her shoulder. She turned with a small frown. "Try not to cuddle and pet Copper too much, Ella."

Ella frowned back. "Why not? He loves it—see?"

As if to prove her point, the tiny kit

licked Ella's cheek.

"Exactly," Mom said. "But it's important not to handle him too much. He's not the same as a kitten or a puppy."

"Yes, he is. You're just as fluffy and cute, aren't you, Copper?" Smiling, Ella tickled the kit on the white patch of fur under his chin.

"Ella, you're not listening. What I'm saying is, he's not a pet." Mom came over and took the kit from her.

Copper let out a tiny, sharp bark.

"Watch out for his sore leg!" Ella cried.

"I am watching out." Mom put Copper back in his unit. "We have to handle him as little as possible. If he gets too used to us, he won't want to go back into the wild."

"Go back?" Ella echoed, surprised.

"Yes. When—if—he gets better. We'll put him back where you found him and hope that he finds his family again."

"Oh!" Ella hadn't thought that far ahead. Put him back by the dark, dangerous river, in the long grass, with all those thorn bushes?

"Yes. Copper is a wild animal. He belongs in the woods and along the riverbank. I thought you realized that."

Ella nodded quickly. "Of course I did," she insisted, trying to sound convincing. "I knew all along we'd have to put him back."

"So don't try to make him a pet. And don't get too attached," Mom warned as she left the cat area.

Tears welled up in Ella's eyes as she

gazed at the fox kit curled up on his blanket. He blinked and licked his lips to taste the last drops of milk.

"Too late!" Ella muttered, brushing away a tear. "I fell in love with you the moment I saw you!"

## Chapter Six
# The Sad Truth

"Why can't you keep him?" Annie asked Ella.

It was Sunday morning in the yard at Animal Magic, and the two girls had brought Buttercup and Chance in from the field. Despite a light drizzle, they had decided to ride.

"Stand still while I tighten your girth," Ella told Buttercup. She'd just told Annie what her mom had said about Copper.

"Why?" Annie asked again.

"Because he's a wild animal," Ella muttered.

"But a lot of people keep wild animals as pets," Annie pointed out, putting on her helmet. "I read in the newspaper about a woman who adopted a lion cub and walked him around on a leash!"

"Hmm." Ella  frowned. "I don't know...." She'd lain awake half the night, worrying about Copper going back to the wild and imagining what it would be like to keep him. *I could house-train him and take him for walks*, she had thought. *He would come to me when I called his name!*

"It would be so cool to give Copper a home!" Annie sighed. She rubbed Buttercup's nose, then put her foot in the stirrup. "That's what Animal Magic is all about, isn't it?"

Ella ignored the question and held the reins while Annie mounted. "About that lion cub on a leash.... What happens when the cub gets too big to be taken for walks?"

"Yeah, I know," Annie agreed. "But that wouldn't happen with Copper, would it? He'll never grow that big."

"Don't go on about it," Ella pleaded. "It's bad enough already."

Glancing down at her friend, Annie saw how miserable she was. "I'm sure your mom knows what she's talking about. There's probably a law against it or something," she sighed. "Only, y'know, people do feed foxes and they get tame. I read about it in—"

"Annie!" Ella groaned.

"Okay, I'm sorry." Pressing her heels against Buttercup's sides, Annie set off across the yard. She waited at the gates while Ella got her bike out of the shed. "Anyway, how is Copper this morning?

Is he getting better?"

Wobbling past Annie and Buttercup on her bike, Ella led the way along the quiet street. "Joel says he had a good night," she reported. "When I saw him this morning, his eyes were bright. He was more lively. In fact, yeah, I think he's slowly getting better, fingers crossed!"

"Did you see Mrs. Brooks this morning?" Dad asked Ella over Sunday afternoon dinner. He was digging into a mountain of roasted red potatoes.

"No—why?" She and Annie had ridden for an hour, taking turns. They'd crossed the river on the road bridge and trotted through the woods beyond the golf course.

"I just wondered what kind of mood she's in," her dad mumbled. "Whoa, these potatoes are hot!"

"She's in a mega-foul mood," Caleb reported. "She stopped me just as I was crossing the yard. She wanted to know when you're going to plant some new lettuce."

"As soon as I've had the chance to

ask Grandpa to drop some off from the garden center," Dad explained. "Until then, we'd better all just be ready for trouble from next door!"

"Uh!" Mom grunted, shaking her head. "Yesterday's little episode with Gordon is the last thing we needed."

"It wasn't Gordon's fault," Caleb reminded them as he glared across the table at Ella. "By the way, I got an email from the Wesleys this morning, confirming that they didn't think he was the goat for them!"

"Don't worry," Mom said. As usual, she refused to get discouraged. "I saw two couples this morning who want to adopt kittens. So Tulip and Ringo are all set up with nice new homes."

"And Copper is getting stronger all

the time," Dad added. "At this rate, we should be able to set him free by the end of next week."

Ella put down her knife and fork and pushed her plate away.

"Not hungry?" her mom asked quietly.

Ella shook her head. "Can I go and help Joel, please?"

Mom nodded. "That would be good. Tell him to take his lunch break while you're over there keeping an eye on things."

Ella slipped out of the house and made her way across the yard. She went into the kennels and then into the cat area, looking for Joel, who was nowhere to be seen. Back on the porch outside the reception area, the noise of a door being bolted inside the stable block told

Ella that Joel was visiting Gordon.

Ella set off toward the stables, then quickly changed her mind. She retraced her steps into the cat area, saying hi to Lily and the rest of the litter, then stopping close to the fox kit's unit. "Hi, Copper," she whispered, longing to pick him up and cuddle him.

*No!* she told herself. *Don't pet him!*

Copper looked up at her with bright eyes. He uncurled himself and stretched. Then he stood gingerly, being careful not to put weight on his injured leg.

"You're beautiful!" Ella breathed. "And so little!"

She gazed at the tiny fox kit's shiny, rust-brown coat with the bright white patch on his chest. His pointed ears were pricked, and his amber eyes shone. With his sore foot raised, Copper tilted his head and gazed back at her.

"So little!" she repeated. Much too small to be set free and made to fend for himself in the long grass and thorn bushes, beside the dangerous water of the fast-flowing river.

"And so helpless," she whispered fearfully. "Oh, Copper, I can't stand it. Why do you have to go?"

## Chapter Seven
# Breaking the Rules

"Did the mail come yet?" Caleb asked when he appeared at breakfast the next morning.

"Nope." Ella had been up for hours. Even though summer vacation had begun, she didn't sleep in late—not when there were dogs to walk, kittens to feed, Copper to take care of…. The list was endless.

Caleb went to the front door to check the box, just in case.

"He's worried about the letter from the Council," Mom guessed. She'd stopped into the house for a coffee after a busy session of canine dentistry. "Jasper's teeth are much better," she told them. "And I've given all the dogs their deworming medicine. When I go back, I'll microchip Coco's litter."

"Can I feed Copper?" Ella asked. She knew it was Joel's day off and jumped at the chance to step in.

"Yes, please." Swallowing the last of her coffee, Mom rushed on ahead.

"You only offered because you want a chance to cuddle him," Caleb scoffed.

"So?" Ella blushed.

"So, he should be learning to eat from a bowl by now, to get ready."

"Ready for what?"

"To go back into the wild, in case you'd forgotten."

Ella's heart sank. "Be quiet, Caleb," she muttered as she dashed after her mom.

"Hey, Copper!" Ella said. She settled the fox kit on her lap.

Copper looked around eagerly for his milk, twitching his ears and flicking his little tail.

"Yes, you know what's coming, don't you? Here you go!"

As Ella slid the dropper between his lips, the kit gulped greedily. Soon, all the milk was gone.

"Good boy!" Ella smiled. She let him lick her fingers. "You're doing really well, you know that?"

Copper's temperature was back to normal. His leg was healing rapidly. For a quick second, Ella gave in to the temptation to hug him.

"Good news!" Caleb burst into the cat area. "I checked the emails, and we've got another inquiry about Gordon!" He broke off as he spotted Ella with Copper.

Guiltily, she put him back in the unit.

"I saw that!" Caleb cried. "You know you're not supposed to pet that kit!"

"I wasn't … I didn't …." Ella shook her head. "Give me a break, Caleb!"

But her brother was still angry with her over Gordon. "You know what Mom said—Copper will never survive in the wild if you handle him all the time."

"I just picked him up to feed him."

"Yeah, well, it'll be your fault if he doesn't survive out there." With that, Caleb stormed out the door.

Ella's heart thumped. She swallowed hard as she gazed down at Copper. "I'm sorry ... I didn't mean ... I mean ... oh, dear!"

The kit gave her a bright stare. He

cocked his head to one side and sat
back on his hind legs, looking just like a
puppy inviting her to play.

"Oh, no!" Ella panicked. "What if
Caleb is right? What if I've ruined your
chances of being able to survive in the
wild?"

Even though it was one of the hardest
things Ella had ever had to do, she
stayed away from Copper all through
Monday and Tuesday. By Wednesday
evening, Mom reported that the kit had
fought off the infection and was now
eating small amounts of kitten food
from a bowl.

"Terrific," Dad said. "When do his
stitches come out?"

"Friday," Mom said. "By the way, when are you going to plant that new lettuce for Linda? She was nagging me about it earlier today."

"As a matter of fact…," Dad began.

They watched him go outside to his van and return with a box of lettuce seedlings.

"I stopped by the garden center on the way home from work," he explained. "Ella, do you want to come next door and help me plant them?"

Ella nodded, desperate to keep busy and not worry about Copper.

Her dad grinned. "Great! Let's go."

"So, what's wrong?" Dad asked as he and Ella knelt side by side in Mrs. Brooks's vegetable garden.

Only Mr. Brooks was home, but he'd

told Dad and Ella to go ahead with the planting.

"Nothing's wrong," Ella fibbed.

"Then why are you so quiet? It's not like you." Dropping a seedling into a small hole, Dad patted the soil around it.

"No reason. I'm fine."

"Did you and Caleb have an argument?"

"No. Well, yeah."

"About Gordon? Is that little incident still on his mind?"

Ella copied her dad and planted another seedling. "Kind of."

They worked for a while in silence, making sure that their rows of seedlings were straight. "Caleb can be a bit of a know-it-all sometimes," her dad began again. "You know, like most big brothers. But don't let him get to you."

"I don't," Ella protested, glad for once to see Mrs. Brooks's car driving through the gates.

Annie jumped out and hurried over. "Hi, Ella! Do you want to take Buttercup out? You can ride first if you want."

"I can't right now. Maybe tomorrow," Ella said, cringing as Annie's mom approached.

Dad looked up from his planting. "These are the best lettuce," he told Mrs. Brooks. "Hand picked and donated by my dad."

Mrs. Brooks inspected the newly planted rows.

"Well?" Dad asked.

"Not bad," Linda acknowledged slowly. "You've planted them nice and straight.

You and Ella have done a good job."

"Thank you, ma'am!" Dad stood up, tipping an imaginary cap and grinning. "So, are we okay?"

Mrs. Brooks sniffed and held her head high. But gradually her face softened into a smile. "Yes, you and Gordon are officially forgiven! In fact, why don't you and Ella come inside for a snack?"

"Wonderful!" Dad sighed. "You hear that, Ella and Annie? You're both witnesses!"

"Don't push it, Mark," Mrs. Brooks warned. "And don't let that goat near my garden ever again!"

"Linda actually said she was sorry for starting up the petition in the first place," Dad told Mom when he and Ella went to look for her in the cat area.

Mom had just admitted a feral cat brought in from an alley on the edge of Crystal Park. The poor creature was thin and scraggly, with a mass of tangled gray fur.

"'Sorry' is not a word I ever expected to hear from Linda's lips," Mom admitted.

"I know. She was talking about it over a cup of coffee after we'd finished planting the lettuce. I almost fell off my chair."

As her parents chatted, Ella sneaked a look at Copper.

As soon as the fox kit spotted her, he tried to climb up the side of his unit.

"No. Stay down, Copper. I'm not allowed to pick you up," she muttered.

"Linda is sorry that she has caused us all this worry about being closed down," Dad went on. "And now she admits she'd never have had the chance to adopt Buttercup and Chance if it hadn't been for Animal Magic."

"Wow," Mom said. "Better late than never, I guess."

"...Stay down, Copper," Ella insisted.

"You resisted him—great job!" her mom said. "Copper's way too cute for his own good."

"Totally," Ella sighed, shaking her head as she tore herself away.

Her dad stared quietly after her. "Aha," he told Mom softly. "Now I know what's gotten into Ella!"

### Chapter Eight
# A Genius Idea

"What's really bothering you?" Ella's dad asked her.

For once, the entire family had gotten together the next evening to relax in front of the television. It was Thursday, and Caleb and Mom wanted to watch a wildlife program that followed the migration of three wild swans across the frozen land of the Canadian Rockies.

"Everything!" Ella admitted.

Her dad sat next to her on the sofa

and put an arm around her shoulder.
"It's Copper, isn't it?" he said quietly.
"That's what's making you miserable."

Ella sighed and nodded.

"Tell me about it," Dad invited gently.

"Shhh!" Caleb said, as he turned up
the volume on the television.

"We won't know how he's doing after
we set him free," Ella answered. "He'll
be all alone. And it's scary out there,
especially at night."

Her dad nodded thoughtfully. "I understand how you feel, but I'm afraid that's life. It's something you're going to have to accept."

"But cars speed down these roads, Dad. Copper might be crossing the road and…." Ella trailed off. "…And even if he doesn't get squished, what will he eat? What if he starves? And what if he has to be alone for the rest of his life?"

"I don't know. But as far as I can see, there's nothing we can do to keep track of a wild animal once we release it."

"So how do they track these swans?" Mom's question showed that she'd been half-listening to their conversation as she watched the television. "Caleb, do you know how they know which bird is which?"

Ella and Dad turned their attention to the screen. They watched the swans gliding on air currents over snow-covered mountains.

"Easy. It told you at the start of the program—they attach tiny radio transmitters to their legs," Caleb explained. "You set a special signal for each bird. The filmmakers receive the signal on a receiver, like a cell phone."

"Clever stuff," Dad said.

Ella stared at the wild birds soaring through the blue sky. "Wow!" she said. "That means they can track them wherever they go!"

"Whoa, just a minute!" Dad warned, worried that Ella was about to come up with one of her infamous ideas.

"No, that's really interesting," Mom

interrupted. "I went to college with a woman named Sue Jones, who tracked a male badger for six months with a tiny transmitter attached to the base of his ear. It was her special project."

"But wait a minute." Dad glanced at Ella. It was too late. Her eyes were gleaming. She was taking in every word.

"We could do that with Copper!" Ella gasped. "We could get a tiny radio and attach it to his ear. Then we'd know exactly where he was!"

"Yeah, but where do we find one of those?" Dad asked. "Don't you need an expert to put it on the animal? Aren't they really expensive?"

"Mom can ask her friend Sue!" Ella exclaimed. She sprang up from the sofa. "Where does Sue live now?"

"Not far. About 20 miles away. I still talk to her from time to time." Mom gave the idea some serious thought. "You know, it might be worth giving her a call."

"Let's call her right now!" Ella insisted. Suddenly, her entire world had turned around. If swans flew over massive mountain ranges giving off radio signals, why couldn't a little fox kit do the same as he roamed through the undergrowth at the bottom of Mrs. Brooks's field?

Mom raised her eyebrows as she glanced at Dad. Caleb had his eyes glued to the television. "It's worth a try," she decided.

"Call now, Mom! Please?" Ella said again, dragging Mom toward the phone.

# A Genius Idea

As they left the
room, she fell
on Caleb
and gave
him a hug.

He shrank
back. "Yuck.
What was
that for?"

"For giving
us a totally cool idea!" Ella cried, and
danced out of the room.

"Joel, could you please bring the light
closer to the table?" It was Friday
morning. Mom, Joel, and Ella were
gathered around the exam table. Ella had
sprayed the surface and wiped it clean

before her mom arrived with Copper.

"That's better. Now we can see exactly what we're doing," Mom said as she pulled on a pair of blue surgical gloves. "Ella, please hold Copper tightly while I quickly take out his stitches."

Gently, Ella held the kit still. He sat quietly, curling his pink tongue across his top lip, his eyes darting every which way.

"Perfect," Mom announced after the job was done. "Now hold on to him while I pierce his ear and put in this sterile pin."

"Your friend Sue told you how this thing works?" Joel asked, watching with interest.

Mom nodded. "I went over to see her early this morning. She was glad to give us the device and explain everything.

## ☘ A Genius Idea ☘

This pin has a small tag that glows in
the dark and sends out a radio signal.
The receiver is that thing that looks
like a cell phone on the shelf over there.
We set it to the right frequency, and
it picks up Copper's whereabouts from
a distance of about a mile away. The
signal gets louder and stronger as you
get closer to the transmitter."

Joel picked up the receiver and turned
it over, looking at it closely.

Quickly, Mom pierced the kit's ear,
almost without him seeming to notice.
The tag was firmly in place.

"See, that didn't hurt," Ella whispered.

"Okay, back into the unit!" Mom
ordered.

Ella whisked the kit from the table
and carried him back into the cat bay.

"Hey, Dixie!" she called out to the stray cat who was now on the Animal Magic website. She placed Copper in his unit. "Until tonight!" she told him.

Tonight was the big night—he was going to be set free.

And now Ella wasn't so afraid for little Copper. It was still a big, scary world out there, and maybe Ella had made him too much of a pet, but when you looked at him, how could you resist?

At least now, with this little tag in his ear, they would know exactly where he was and that he was safe!

"See you later, Copper," Ella whispered.

She closed the door of the cat area with her fingers crossed, half-afraid, half-excited about what lay ahead.

## Chapter Nine
# A Magical Good-bye

"Don't go near Gordon!" Caleb warned as Ella went out into the yard.

She'd left Joel and her mom to figure out exactly how the radio receiver worked and had bumped into Caleb.

"Why not?" Ella wanted to know.

"A man named Eric is on his way to see him right now. And you know what happened the last time with the Wesleys."

"Okay, okay—don't rub it in!" Ella laughed. No way was grumpy Caleb going to spoil Copper's special day.

"Just don't go near him with sprays and brushes, okay?" Caleb grumbled.

"Oh, please, let me brush him and make him pretty!" she said teasingly, advancing toward the stables.

Caleb blocked Ella's way. "Very funny!" he muttered as a muddy truck turned into the yard.

Out stepped an elderly man in a worn tweed jacket and boots.

"Hello, er—Eric?" Caleb said uncertainly.

"Where's this goat of yours?" The visitor got right down to business, marching into the stable and taking a long, hard look at Gordon.

"Scary man!" Ella mouthed at Caleb behind the visitor's back. She saw a black-and-white collie sitting patiently in the truck.

"Yeah," Caleb whispered back.

They followed him inside.

Boldly, Eric went up to Gordon and ran a hand through his silky coat. Then to Gordon's surprise, the man slid his fingers into the goat's mouth and checked his teeth.

"Hmm," Eric said.

Gordon snickered uneasily as the visitor firmly closed his mouth, then picked up one foot at a time to inspect his hooves.

"Good boy, Gordon!" Caleb muttered nervously. Any second now, the goat was going to knock the man to the ground with a mighty kick.

"Nice pedigree," Eric reported. "Good condition. Nice job, buddy."

"Nice job, who? Me or Gordon?" Caleb whispered to Ella.

She shrugged. Didn't Eric know the risk he was taking if he pushed Gordon around like that?

But Gordon stood meekly as he had his feet lifted and his mouth inspected a second time.

"The thing is, I don't know if I really need a goat right now," the man explained as he came out of Gordon's stall.

Gordon stood with a puzzled expression. Ella thought he was probably wondering why he hadn't managed to get in a quick head-butt.

"I have a small herd of goats at a farm on the other side of the valley," Eric told Ella and Caleb. "My son, Josh, saw this one on your website and said I should come and take a look."

"A goat farm?" Caleb checked out the visitor. Now the muddy truck and the patient dog made sense. "Hey, Gordon, doesn't that sound cool?"

Eric frowned and jutted out his bottom lip. "I'm not saying for certain that I'll take him off your hands. I only came to give him a quick look."

Caleb and Ella nodded and exchanged hopeful glances. They'd definitely gotten over their first impression of Eric as Mr. Scary.

"As I said, I don't really need another billy goat. The one I have, Tyson, is a handful as it is."

Ella thought fast. "Yes, but Gordon isn't hard to handle," she burst out. "You saw for yourself. He's really gentle!"

Caleb's eyes almost popped out of his head at this, but he didn't say a word.

"And like you said, he's in great condition," Ella added.

In the background, Gordon let out a bray to tell them that he knew they were talking about him.

Eric nodded and strode back to his truck. "Let me think about it and talk with Josh," he told them as he sat behind the wheel.

"I'll be in touch," he said, starting the engine and pulling out of the yard.

"Will he or won't he?" Ella asked. She'd done her best to convince Eric to give Gordon what sounded like a wonderful new home.

Caleb shrugged. "Fingers crossed," he muttered.

"They're already crossed," Ella replied, holding up both hands. "For Copper and now for Gordon. Let's hope that everything works out okay!"

That evening, Ella and Mom went alone to the place on the riverbank where Ella had found Copper exactly a week earlier.

Ella carried him across the field in a

lightweight pet carrier, following the beam of her mom's flashlight. "Mom, did you bring the radio receiver?" she double-checked.

"In my jacket pocket," Mom replied as they reached the fence. "Here, let me hold Copper while you climb over."

"Did you test the battery?" Ella asked.

"Yes."

"What about the transmitter? Are you sure it's working?"

Following Ella over the fence, Mom landed on the sloping riverbank. The flashlight wobbled and wavered across the dark, rapid water. "No more questions, Ella. Everything's ready. Let's just do it!"

Ella took a deep breath and placed the carrier carefully on the ground. She

crouched beside it and opened the door.
Inside, Copper sat with his pointed ears
pricked, his fiery eyes glinting in the
flashlight beam.

"Come out, Copper, it's time to go,"
she whispered.

But the fox kit seemed to be in no
hurry. He lifted one paw and licked it,
then the other.

"He doesn't want to leave. Should I lift
him out?" Ella asked.

"No. Let him do it himself. Wait a
minute while I shut off the light and
turn on the receiver."

With the press of a button on the
small handset, a clear beeping sound
broke the night's silence.

Inside the carrier, Copper pricked
his ears, then crept forward until he

teetered at the edge. As he picked up
scents in the grass, he ducked his head
and sniffed hard.

"Good boy!" Mom encouraged.

"Look, the little tag does glow in the
dark!" Ella breathed, watching the small
green light attached to Copper's ear.

Growing braver, the kit ventured out
into the long grass. He seemed alert,
listening to every swish and crackle of
his surroundings.

The signal beeped as Copper took his
first steps back into nature.

"So far, so good," Mom whispered.

Ella crouched quietly, watching
Copper dig at the soft ground with one
of his front paws. He sniffed again, then
trotted on a few steps.

*Come back!* her heart said. But her
head knew he must go.

Beep-beep. The signal sounded loud
and clear.

Copper padded along the riverbank, half-hidden by the thorn bushes. Then he stopped and turned to look right at Ella. He paused and tilted his head to one side.

*It's like he's asking me a question*, Ella thought, her heart beating fast. *Is it okay if I go now?*

"He's saying thank you and good-bye," Mom whispered.

"Good-bye, Copper!" Ella muttered, her heart racing. He looked calm and happy out here, ready to continue on with his old life in the wild.

The fox kit swished his tail. His eyes glinted. Then he turned and disappeared down the slope.

## Chapter Ten
# Tracking Copper

Ella slept badly that night, tossing and turning and replaying in her mind the moment when Copper had turned his head to say good-bye. A magical, sad moment in the moonlight.

She got up early to turn on the radio receiver and listen.

Beep-beep-beep. Copper's signal came through loud and clear.

Sighing, Ella went into the cat area. Animal Magic seemed empty without

Copper, but Dixie the alley cat was meowing loudly, so Ella gave her a small bowl of food.

"Ella, are you in there?" Annie's voice floated in through the reception area.

"Coming!" she replied, going to greet her friend.

"How did it go last night?" Annie asked.

"Good. Copper trotted off along the riverbank, no problem."

"Did he look scared?"

"No. Pretty confident, actually."

"And are you getting a signal?" Annie pestered. She wanted to hear every detail about the fox kit's release.

Ella took out the receiver and turned it on. "Listen!"

Beep-beep-beep.

Annie grinned. "How great is that! But sad, too."

Ella nodded. "I miss him," she confessed.

"I know. But Ella, guess what? Mom called Mr. Winters at the Council again, saying she definitely wanted to withdraw the petition against Animal Magic!"

Ella sat down on a stool with a loud gasp.

"I know. I couldn't believe it either."

"How come she's done it again?" Ella asked.

"It's Buttercup and Chance," Annie explained. "Ever since we adopted them, she's been feeling worse and worse about wanting to have you closed down. She kept talking to Dad about it and in the end she called again."

"So did they say we can stay open?"

"Well," Annie began. "Not exactly. It turns out that Mr. Winters reminded Mom it wasn't as simple as that."

"Ahh," Ella said quietly.

"He said a lot of other people had signed the petition. And anyway, it wasn't up to him."

"So who is it up to?"

"The entire Council. And they've already decided," Annie told her.

"So?" As quickly as Ella's hopes rose, they fell again.

"Mr. Winters wouldn't tell Mom over the phone. But he said the letter to your mom and dad was definitely in the mail."

"Well, it didn't come this morning,"

Ella muttered. "And it's Sunday
tomorrow."

"So it'll be here on Monday." Annie
held up her hand with her fingers
crossed. "Here's hoping that it's a yes for
Animal Magic."

"I don't have enough fingers," Ella
sighed. "Come on. Let's go and walk
Jasper."

### Chapter Eleven
# A Family Reunion

Walk the dogs, feed the cats, muck out Gordon's stall. The list of Saturday jobs went on and on.

"Take a break, Ella," her mom insisted. It was early evening, and Ella was flopped on a chair in the reception area, looking tired. "Go over to the house and grab a sandwich."

"Can I take the receiver with me?" All day Ella had kept it by her side, reassured by the faint beep-beep of

Copper's signal.

Mom nodded and smiled. "Copper is doing okay, believe me!"

"I still want to listen," Ella insisted. She trudged across the yard, kicked off her boots in the kitchen doorway, and went inside.

"You didn't go near Gordon, did you?" Caleb asked suspiciously. He, too, was refueling with a giant ham and cheese sandwich.

"I had to muck him out," Ella retorted, washing her hands before she cut into the loaf of bread.

"Did you lock his door all the way?"

"Yeah, yeah. Anyway, did Eric call back?"

"Not yet." Casually Caleb picked up the radio handset. As he fiddled with the volume, the beeping sound stopped all of a sudden.

"Hey, what happened?" Ella took the receiver from him. "What did you do?"

"Nothing. It just stopped. Give it back. Let me try again."

"We lost the signal!" Ella wailed. She felt panic rise inside her.

Caleb tapped buttons without success. "Yeah, we lost it," he agreed at last.

"Caleb, you don't think…?" Ella couldn't put into words a terrible idea that had come into her head.

"What? That something bad has happened to Copper?" Caleb frowned. He remembered the wild swans flying over the mountains. One of them had stopped transmitting, and then they'd found him … out of range, and dead!

Ella could hardly breathe. "We've got to do something! Try again, Caleb. The transmitter can't fall off, can it?"

"No way. Ella, I think we should go and look for Copper."

"Yes!" Ella agreed. "Right now. Come on, Caleb. Bring the receiver!" Slipping her boots back on, she ran outside and headed for the river.

Copper could have drowned! He could have been run over, chased, even killed!

Ella's imagination ran wild as she and Caleb sprinted across Buttercup's field.

"Still no signal," Caleb reported as they reached the spot on the riverbank where Ella and Mom had released the kit into the wild.

Ella knelt down in the long grass. She felt like crying, but she forced herself to keep searching.

"Which way did he go?" Caleb asked.

"Toward the bridge." Ella pointed in that direction. "We're never going to find his tracks, though. He's too small and light."

"Let's try," Caleb insisted. He stepped carefully along the bank, looking for tiny pawprints in the soft mud.

"It's hopeless," Ella sighed as they reached the bridge. Still the receiver was silent. There was no sign of life from Copper.

"We need to keep trying," Caleb insisted. "Maybe Copper went out of range—you know, too far away for the receiver to pick up his signal."

"He couldn't have. He's too little to travel almost a mile in one day."

"You're probably right. And the signal did get cut off suddenly. It didn't fade and then stop."

"So which way now?" Ella asked miserably.

"Over the bridge," Caleb decided.

With fading hope, Ella and Caleb crossed the old stone bridge.

"Left or right?" Caleb asked.

Ella looked to the right, at the golf course with its smooth, open greens. To the left were the woods. If Copper had any sense, he would seek shelter there. "Left," she decided.

On they went in the failing light, into the shadow of the tall trees. Step by step Ella grew more certain that something terrible had happened to Copper.

"This is all my fault," she moaned. "If I hadn't petted him and made him tame, he would have stood a better chance."

"Knock it off, Ella!" Caleb said gruffly. Then he spoke more kindly. "Forget what I said earlier. This isn't your fault. Out here in the wild, it's just luck whether or not a fox kit makes it."

Ella sniffed, then listened to the sounds all around, peering between the wide trunks of two trees. "What was that? I thought I saw something move."

"It's nothing," Caleb decided, staring at the handset and turning the volume to maximum. "But hang on a minute— I think we're picking up a signal again!"

Beep-beep, beep-beep.

"Yes!" Ella gasped. "It's faint, but it's there!"

"This way!" Caleb said, setting off in the direction where the signal grew louder.

Not dead. Not attacked and injured. Still alive.... *Please!*

Now each step took them closer to Copper. The signal strengthened as they sprinted between trees, over logs, and through thick bushes.

"Shhh!" Caleb warned. In the gloom of the woods, they'd picked up the loudest signal yet. "Let's stop and watch!"

Ella and Caleb crouched down behind the mossy trunk of a fallen tree.

Beep-beep-beep. The signal didn't weaken, but grew stronger.

Shadows seemed to move as their eyes played tricks. "Look!" Ella leaped up, convinced that she'd seen a small animal hiding behind a tree trunk.

"Squirrel!" Caleb whispered, pulling her back down.

Beep-beep. The signal of hope.

Then at last it happened. A shape appeared out of a hole in the ground. Amber eyes glinted.

"Oh!" Ella sighed. This time she stayed hidden behind the tree trunk.

A grown fox came into view. They could just see her—pointed ears, sleek body, and furry tail. She looked this way and that way, sniffed the air, and waited.

Then a baby fox tumbled out of the half-hidden hole, and another. Two kits following their mother.

"Which one is Copper?" Caleb whispered.

"Neither," Ella answered. She was waiting for a kit with a transmitter glowing with a dim green light.

And there it was! A third baby emerged from the hole, skipping quickly after the other two, shaking himself and yawning.

Beep-beep-beep. The signal sounded louder than ever.

"Copper found his family!" Ella sighed.

"Or they found him," Caleb added.

"Whichever." Ella didn't care. All that mattered was that Copper was alive and well ... and back where he belonged!

"The mystery is solved!" Mom smiled broadly as the family sat down to a late dinner that night. "You lost the signal because Copper was in his den!"

"And the transmitter doesn't work underground," Dad explained to Caleb and Ella. "We'll have to remember that."

"But we saw him!" Ella cried. "He has brothers and sisters. He has a mom again!"

"Wonderful," her dad said.

"And it was like nothing bad ever happened." Still bubbling with excitement, Ella ignored her food. "His mom watched over him and kept him in line."

"As moms do," Dad grinned when Mom told Ella to finish her dinner.

"We watched them for about 10 minutes," Caleb reported. "Then they wandered off between the trees. You could still see them in the moonlight."

"So beautiful!" Ella sighed.

"So sometimes what we do here at Animal Magic is not about finding homes," Mom pointed out.

"Sometimes it's about freedom," Dad said, finishing her thought.

"Speaking of finding a new home," Ella and Caleb's dad remembered. "Eric Greene called when you were out. He says he's talked things over with his son, and they'll be glad to take Gordon off our hands. They can pick him up tomorrow."

Ella and Caleb jumped up from the table and gave each other a high five.

"Awesome!" Caleb said.

"Where are you going?" her mom protested as Ella headed for the door.

"To tell Gordon!" she insisted, sprinting across the yard and flinging open the stable door.

Laughing, Dad and Mom followed their excited son and daughter.

"Gordon, you're going to live on a farm!" Ella announced.

The goat looked up in surprise from his dinner of oats and barley.

Caleb, Mom, and Dad smiled and watched quietly.

But Ella clapped her hands and jumped up and down. "Copper has found his family, and Gordon has a new home," she said. "Is this a great day, or what!"

Have you read...

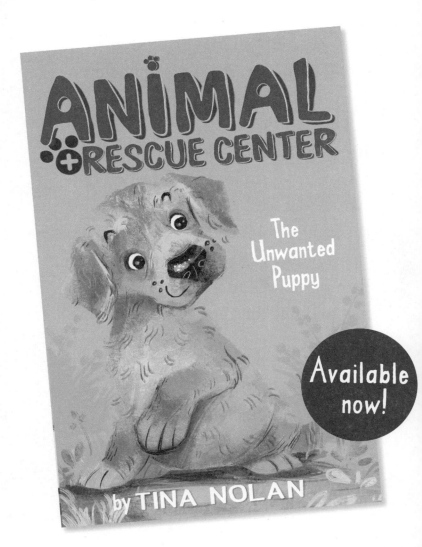

ANIMAL RESCUE CENTER

The Unwanted Puppy

Available now!

by TINA NOLAN

# ANIMAL
# RESCUE CENTER

The
Home-alone
Kitten

Available
now!

by TINA NOLAN